This book belongs to:

_____

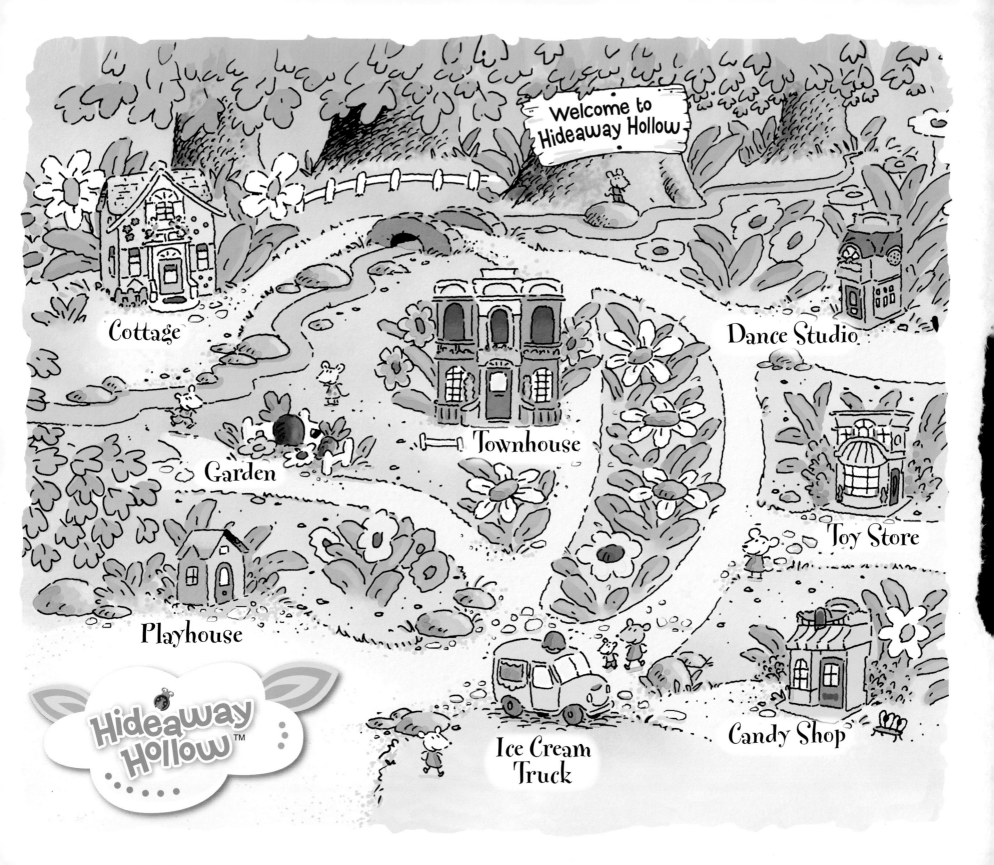

A Surprise for Stella Squeak

Fisher-Price

By Colleen Tomasso
Illustrated by Mike Gordon
and Carl Gordon

In a charming place where the footpath ends,
you'll find Stella Squeak helping all her friends!

When Max flooded Mari Gold's garden, Stella
helped them throw a pool party in the puddles.

When Tommy Treats got his truck stuck
in the muck, Stella helped him pull it out.

And when baby Bella fell, Stella kissed her boo-boos and bandaged her up.

"Let's plan a party for Stella!" said Maddy. "She's always helping her friends. She deserves a nice surprise."

"Surprise!" squeaked Bella.
"Surprise!" squeaked Max.

At the Candy Shop, Maddy said, "We need treats
for a—oh, hi Stella. What are you doing here?"

"I'm helping Candice stock the shelves," said Stella.

"Don't these cheddar lollipops look yummy?"

"We'll take all the lollipops!" exclaimed Maddy.

"Can I help?" asked Stella.

"No, thank you, we're fine," said Maddy. "Bye-bye!"

"Bye-bye!" squeaked Bella.
"Bye-bye!" squeaked Max.

Next, they headed to Tommy Treats' Truck for the tastiest treats in town.

"Are you here for a fabulous frozen frosty treat?" asked Tommy.

"Yes!" said Maddy. "We're planning a—
oh, hi Stella! What are you doing here?"

"I'm helping Tommy scoop ice cream," said Stella. "He's got all of my favorites—cheddariffic sundaes, hunka-chunka cheddar ice cream, orange-you-cheddar frozen pops ... yum!"

"We'll take some of each kind!" exclaimed Maddy.

"Can I help?" asked Stella.

"No, thank you, we're fine," said Maddy. "See you, Stella!"

"See you, Stella!" squeaked Bella.

"See you, Stella!" squeaked Max.

At Mari Gold's garden, Maddy said, "We need
some goodies for the—oh, hi Stella. It's you again!"
"I'm helping Mari Gold weed her garden," said Stella.

Mari Gold had bunches of beautiful flowers,
cartons of carrots, and pails of peas ready to go.

"All my favorites!" said Stella. "Except for the peas."

"We'll take them all," said Maddy. "But no peas, please!"

"No peas!" squeaked Bella.
"No peas!" squeaked Max.

"Can I help?" asked Stella.

"Yes, please! Could you deliver everything at six o'clock?" said Maddy.

"Of course!" said Stella. "See you then!"

Maddy was so happy. Her plans for the party were falling into place! And Stella was glad she could finally help her best friend.

"This sure is a *lot* of stuff!" said Stella.

"SURPRISE!" shouted Stella's friends. "We planned a big party just for you!"

"It's a party to say 'thank you' for all the nice things you do!"

"Whoops!" said a very surprised Stella.

"Don't worry, Stella," said Maddy. "We'll help clean up this mess!"

"Thank you, thank you!" Stella squeaked. "I'm so happy
to have all of you as friends. This is such a nice surprise!"

"Surprise!" squeaked Bella.

"Surprise!" squeaked Max.

The End

Fisher-Price®

Edited by Maureen Purcell
Marketing Direction by Kathy Cox
Art Direction by Marcia Ganes
Creator of Hideaway Hollow product line-
Mary Mastrosimone-Gese